Dear Parent:

Your child's love of readin

Every child learns to read in a different way
speed. Some go back and forth between reading levels and read favorite books again and again. Others read through each level in order. You can help your young reader improve and become more confident by encouraging his or her own interests and abilities. From books your child reads with you to the first books he or she reads alone, there are I Can Read Books for every stage of reading:

SHARED READING
Basic language, word repetition, and whimsical illustrations, ideal for sharing with your emergent reader

BEGINNING READING
Short sentences, familiar words, and simple concepts for children eager to read on their own

READING WITH HELP
Engaging stories, longer sentences, and language play for developing readers

READING ALONE
Complex plots, challenging vocabulary, and high-interest topics for the independent reader

I Can Read Books have introduced children to the joy of reading since 1957. Featuring award-winning authors and illustrators and a fabulous cast of beloved characters, I Can Read Books set the standard for beginning readers.

A lifetime of discovery begins with the magical words **"I Can Read!"**

Visit www.icanread.com for information on enriching your child's reading experience.

Baby Shark and the Balloons

 For information address HarperCollins Children's Books, a division of HarperCollins Publishers, 195 Broadway, New York, NY 10007.

www.icanread.com

ISBN 978-0-06-296584-4

---

19 20 21 22 23 LSCC 10 9 8 7 6 5 4 3 2 1

First Edition

pinkfong BABY SHARK and the Balloons

HARPER
An Imprint of HarperCollins*Publishers*

Baby Shark Family & Friends

Baby Shark

Mommy Shark

Daddy Shark

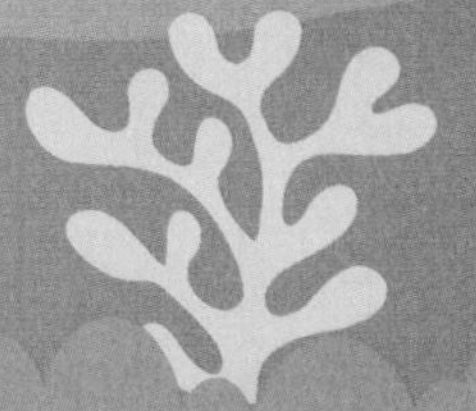

Baby Turtle

Baby Seahorse

Baby Whale

Grandma Shark

Grandpa Shark

Baby Shark is looking
for his friends.
Where could they be?

Baby Shark is very bored.
"I am so bored!" he says.
"Bored as can be."

But look, Baby Shark!
It's a treasure chest.

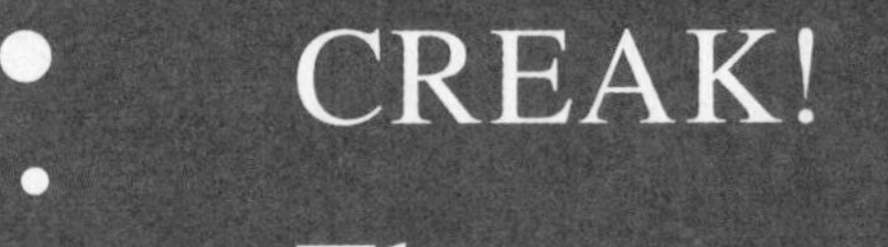

CREAK!

The treasure chest opens.

Balloons float out.

“Wow!” Baby Shark says.
“Colorful balloons!”

Baby Shark ties
the balloons to his tail.

"Wheeee!" he says.
"Balloons are so fun."

Hold on!

Who is that on the coral?

It's Baby Turtle.

Baby Turtle is going too fast!

"Ouch!" she says.

"Gosh!" Baby Shark says.
"Are you okay, Baby Turtle?"

Baby Shark puts a bandage
on Baby Turtle's boo-boo.
Then he gives her
a yellow balloon.

Baby Turtle feels much better.
"Hooray!" she says.

Baby Shark and Baby Turtle sing and giggle together.

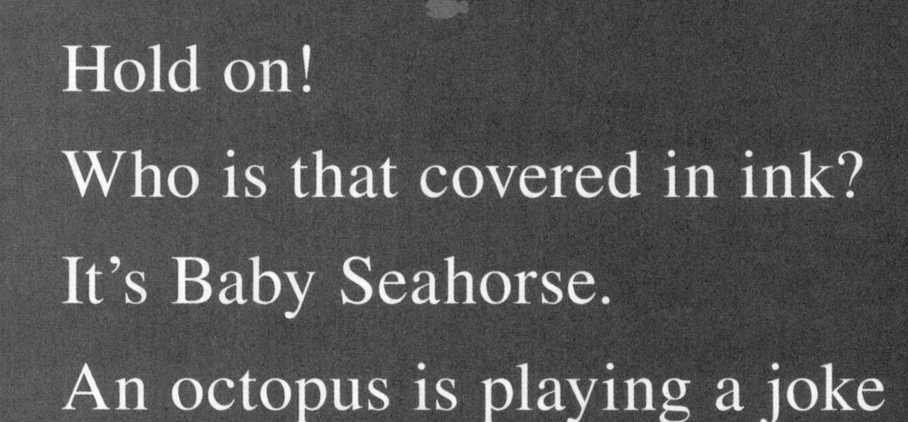

Hold on!
Who is that covered in ink?
It's Baby Seahorse.
An octopus is playing a joke
on him.

"Gosh!" Baby Shark says.
"Are you okay, Baby
Seahorse?"

The friends wash the ink
off Baby Seahorse.
Then they give
him a red balloon.

Baby Seahorse feels better.
“I am all clean!” he says.

The friends sing
and giggle together.

Hold on!
Who is that on the seesaw?
It's Baby Whale!

Baby Whale feels left out.

“I am so lonely!” he says.

“Gosh!” Baby Shark says.
“Are you okay, Baby Whale?”

The friends sit on the seesaw.
Then they give
him a green balloon.

Hooray!

The friends sing
and giggle together.

Friends and balloons
always bring smiles.
"So much for being bored!"
Baby Shark cheers.